The Revelationer

How to Share the Joy and Hope
About the Love of your Life
In a New and Exciting
Way

Reverend Fred Rundell

Xulon PRESS

The Revelationer
by Fred Rundell

Illustrations by Jonathan Allen

Printed in the United States of America

Library of Congress Control Number: 2003100511
ISBN 1-591605-87-3

All Scripture is taken from the King James Version of the Bible, Copyright © 1972 by Thomas Nelson Inc.

Words in *italics* within scriptures are author's emphasis and are not found in original text.

Xulon Press
10640 Main Street
Suite 204
Fairfax, VA 22030
(703) 934-4411
XulonPress.com

To order additional copies, call 1-866-909-BOOK (2665).

TABLE OF CONTENTS

INTRODUCTION

The call of this book is for Christians, who are the true witnesses, to share the best event that has ever happened in their lives. They will be able to share God's plan of salvation in a new and exciting way throughout the earth. It is also to restore the original meanings and purposes of some of the more critical truths of God's Word from our minds to our hearts. This book will bring a new fire and a clearer focus of the glory of God. It will prepare the Bride of Christ for marriage with the Lamb and restore the joy of our salvation.

Our commission from Jesus Christ is <u>to go</u> and teach all nations about Him. As witnesses we will use the Word of God to bring the mighty and awesome power of the Gospel to a generation that has never heard how loving and gracious our Heavenly Father is. We have known the power in our lives but have been shut down because of the enemy's lies in this country. It is time to rejoice. God has shown us a new and biblical way of sharing the greatest event that has ever happened to us as believers. (Details are in the rest of the book.) You do not have to be a great evangelist or teacher to be able to share your personal testimony about the Lord

Jesus Christ. You just have to be willing.

We are all witnesses to the truths of the living Word that has given us eternal life. As witnesses, we must stand and testify of what we have seen. In the kingdom of God, we cannot plead the fifth amendment and be silent. It's not in the Holy Scriptures. Deep down in the depths of our hearts, we love to share about the love of our lives, Jesus Christ. We love to speak the words of eternal life. We yearn to sow the seeds of God's Holy Word. This book will give you many great opportunities to talk freely about the one you love. The Holy Scriptures say, "Let God arise, let his enemies be scattered" (Ps. 68:1). It is time to go.

CHAPTER 1

REVELATIONER

W ord games. The enemy of our soul loves to play word games. He started at the beginning of creation and still plays them today. "The god of this world hath blinded the minds of them which believe not, lest the light of the glorious Gospel of Christ, who is the image of God, should shine unto them" (2 Cor. 4:4). In the Garden of Eden, the adversary deceived Eve by twisting the Word of God and the fall of man came because of Adam's sin (see Genesis Chapter 3). The father of lies, Satan, tried to do the twist again in the wilderness temptations of our Lord Jesus Christ (see Luke Chapter 4). Jesus Christ answered back with the true and accurate Word of God. Satan has been doing the twist on the truth for a very long time, and we must realize he is still doing it today.

The Holy Scriptures reveal the power of God's Word. We must speak it and release the most powerful sound in the universe. "Death and life are in the power of the tongue" (Prov. 18:21). "A wholesome tongue is a tree of life" (Prov. 15:4). We know that "the Word of God is quick, and power-ful, and sharper than any twoedged sword" (Heb. 4:12), but we seem to hesitate to speak the Word. Some people are ashamed to speak the truth. When you learn to speak the Word of God, the power of His Word will be released. The Word of God brings strength to the weak, healing to the sick, deliverance to the captive and life to the dead. They are His Words and they have the power to create. They must be spoken from us or else the deaf will never hear the words of hope.

Do you believe it is possible for someone to approach you and ask you for the Gospel? Do you believe it is possible that you could tell them God's plan of salvation without using the following words—Jesus, sin, repent, church, or God—and still be speaking the Words of God to their hearts? The Lord has shown me many different slogans and has blessed me with a very good Christian artist to put attractive designs on shirts and hats that will have people ask you, "What is the Revelation?" (The web site listed at the back of the book lists the different shirts available for purchase.) As you will see, it is endless as to what can be said as you witness the plan of salvation. The point is that people will ask you what the revelation is. The following pages are just the start of the new and exciting way to witness to a lost and dead generation.

This is one of the examples of how to share the great plan of salvation to anyone who asks. Imagine you are sitting on a bench in a mall and you have a shirt on with the slogan that reads, "Revelation...Got it?" Someone sits next to you and asks, "What's the Revelation?" You then begin to share the following:

> "Long ago, in the beginning of time, the Creator of the Universe created the first man and woman. He created a unique creation when he made the first man and woman, in that He gave them free will or choice to obey Him or disobey Him. He created them so

unique (hold up your finger) that even unto this day, no man or woman has the same fingerprint. That's how special each and every person is to Him. His lovingkindness is great toward all of His creation and He wants to spend time with them. Unfortunately, one day the first man and woman chose to disobey Him and they died spiritually. The Creator could not have disobedience in His presence, so a penalty had to be applied. Because of this, a separation occurred in the spirit and physical death was birthed."

"The Creator longed for His creation to be restored to the place they once had, so He made a plan to restore His fallen creation. About 2000 years ago, the Creator came in the flesh and walked among us to pay the penalty of death so that restoration could be fulfilled in all who made covenant with Him. One of His names that He was known by was Immanuel. He came in the flesh and lived the perfect life. He healed many, performed great miracles, and showed us how to live the life that the Creator wants us to live. He died so that all our faults, shortcomings, and bad behaviors are totally forgiven. In His death, He paid the penalty for our disobedience. When He rose from the dead after three days and three nights in the grave, He gave us victory over death. Those who have entered the true covenant with Him now live life in that power and are totally restored to their right relationship with the Creator. They have peace and joy in all situations because the Creator sent His only begotten Son to

redeem them from the penalty of death, and
they now have everlasting life. Have you
ever heard about how the Creator of all
humbled himself in human form in order for
us to have new life in our soul? You may
have heard of Him by His other name, Jesus
Christ."

I could go on, but I think you see my point. I have just
presented the Gospel of Christ to you. I am sure that real
Christians recognized it right away. Unbelievers may have
heard the true Gospel for the first time. (*Gospel* means
"good news"). So many people have a twisted view of real
Christianity that it is hard to share the truth with strangers,
because as soon as "Christ" or "being a Christian" is
mentioned, walls go up and it is difficult to talk heart to
heart. For those who are really born again, we want to share
the best event that has ever happened to us. In our hearts we
want everyone to know about the great salvation of our
Lord, but it's discouraging when we cannot get past the lies
of the enemy. If you have another situation and your time is
limited, you could use this example:

"About 2000 years ago, the Creator of the
universe came down in human form and
walked among us in order to restore us back
to Him. His name was Immanuel. He lived a
perfect life, paid the penalty for our disobedience, and rose from the dead after three
days and three nights. All those who accept
His covenant will have a new heart with
great peace and joy in this life and have eternal life with their Creator. Have you ever
heard this before?"

There will be some instances when you may not have time or feel led to share the plan of salvation with a certain individual. In those instances, give the person the hard truth. It could be, "Jesus is returning soon and it's time to repent or perish." It could be your personal testimony. You could share what you were going through and how your eyes were opened to everlasting life. (Remember not to use the key words until after you are done with your testimony.) The sharing could be anything the Holy Spirit leads. Tell them it's "the best news they could ever hear," and then arrange to tell them later. Let the Holy Spirit lead you and great answers will come out of your heart that you have never thought of before. Remember, these are divine appointments that the Most High has set before you. You may not even have to open the conversation because others will ask you about the "Revelation."

The key to witnessing in this way is to use alternative words to share the Gospel. It's still the truth, but they are words that are not familiar to them. The lost have been trained to block out anyone who uses words like "Jesus," "God," "church," "Christ," "sin," "saved," "repent," "the cross," or "born again." So we will use words like "Immanuel," "disobedience," "covenant," "lovingkindness," "Creator," and "restored." It will temporarily confuse the lying spirits because they have not prepared lies for those words. Most unbelievers have never heard the name of Immanuel (God is with us). When you get to the part about Immanuel, share all about Jesus' life and purpose. We know that this is one of His names, so use it as you begin to witness. It is important to be led of the Holy Spirit and share what the Spirit leads. Be careful not to get on any "rabbit trails" that will distract from the message of salvation. The purpose is to tell of the great plan of salvation that God has provided. The lies of the enemy can be cleansed in the discipling process. Just stick to the plan of salvation. At the end of the witnessing, ask them if they want to repent and make covenant with the living God through Jesus Christ, our Lord and Savior. The beginning of the power of God in their lives is when they repent and accept Jesus Christ as Lord.

I know there will be some who say that we should mention Jesus up front and not hide it. From all that I have studied about Paul's speeches in the Book of Acts, he covered the history of the Jews and God's covenant and then mentioned Jesus (Acts 13 and 17). That was wisdom. He was able to show more of Christ through Holy Scripture and history than pointing out the Messiah. The Jews would not have listened if he had mentioned Jesus as the Messiah first. Look at the revolts that happened when he finally did show Jesus as the Messiah. In other situations (Acts 22 and 26) Paul shared his personal conversion and testimony with unbelievers. The testimony of Jesus Christ in your life can never be disputed by others. That is why your testimony is so powerful to share. It is God's Word alive and at work in this world.

Most of this present generation has never heard about the beginning of creation. They have been told they are accidents that happened and they were lucky to come out of the caves. They have never been told how special and unique they are. They are loved beyond measure but must repent of their sins and be set free from them. By revealing Jesus Christ at the end, you will be able to share the Gospel in a way as never before. This will let you put the seed of the Word of God into their hearts before they realize it. That is exciting because every seed we plant has great potential. We could change this country back to God and true Christianity one heart at a time. That's true revival! The main idea is to share the Gospel as far as you can using similar words of God and without mentioning Jesus, which will keep their guard down for 5-10 minutes. This will give you the unique opportunity to share the real Gospel of Christ before they can put their walls up.

I want to point out that at this time I believe that this is a calling to those who have a deep desire to share the Gospel in a new and powerful way. This is a call for true Christians to stand up and walk in the light and not be ashamed of the Gospel of Jesus Christ. By sharing our testimony and keeping God's commandments, we will separate ourselves from the faults of Western Christianity. It is a way for us to stand up and bring glory to the living God (see Chapter 10). These are divine appointments that the Lord will bring to you every time you wear one of the "Revelationer" shirts. It will be fun and exciting to see the Lord move lost souls into your path so that you can share the Gospel with them.

Many people will recognize that you are a Christian either during or after you have finished sharing the Gospel. This is a great opportunity to share your personal testimony with them. I know when you share the transformation that Jesus did in your life, they cannot argue as strongly against it. It's the power of the Gospel. This is when you can share as a Revelationer that you have the testimony of Jesus Christ and you keep the commandments of God. It is by faith and through His grace that you have this testimony and strength. Do not let pride come in. Stay humble in the Lord. If the person is a Christian, ask him if he wants to be a part of the "Revelationary War." We have a whole country to witness to and are going to have lots of fun doing so.

Truly, the point of the Revelationers is to spread the Gospel into hearts that need to hear it. It's not about deceitfulness. "Behold, I send you forth as sheep in the midst of wolves: be ye therefore wise as serpents, and harmless as doves" (Matt. 10:16). We are to ask for wisdom. We cannot afford to let pride contaminate the revelation effort by anyone thinking they are better than other Christians. However, the Revelationer idea is for you if you have a burden to touch more people with Christ and if you are tired of being shut off from sharing because of all the negative faults of Western Christianity. If you are looking for a window of opportunity to share the best thing that has ever happened to you and not be cut off in the first minute, I believe God has revealed a way to do just that. Be a Revelationer and let the joy of serving the Lord be upon you!

When someone asks you about the revelation, it is very important for you to realize that this is a <u>divine appointment</u> brought before you by the Most High. It is extremely important to acknowledge that the Lord has entrusted you with this special opportunity. You should be prayed up and ready to share. "Preach the word; be instant in season, out of season; reprove, rebuke, exhort with all longsuffering and doctrine" (2 Tim. 4:2).

Many Christians believe that only evangelists should try to save the lost. The Holy Scriptures say: "Therefore if any man be in Christ, he is a new creature: old things are passed away; behold, all things are become new, and all things are of God, who hath reconciled us to himself by Jesus Christ, and hath *given to us the ministry of reconciliation"* (2 Cor. 5:17-18). (This will be discussed in detail in a later chapter.) The point here is that if you have been "born again," you should be sharing the Gospel because that is your ministry. You don't have to be in full-time ministry or go overseas on missions to share about our Lord Jesus Christ. You just need to be willing and obey the Holy Spirit as the divine appointments come.

The following pages present truths that the Lord wants to use to strengthen the Body of Christ and renew our covenant with new heart truths. (Read on and you will know what heart truths are.) These heart truths will be in bold print throughout the book. Meditate on these until they get deep into your heart, not just your mind.

Be a part of the Revelationary War. Time is short and the

trumpet is ready to sound. The harvest is ready, so let the laborers be strong and prepared for the greatest harvest ever seen in the world. The latter rain is upon us and the work must begin. Go.

CHAPTER 2

GOING DEEPER

There is a time in our lives when we must get serious. There is a time when we must get focused. There is a time when we must be sold out and consumed with the task at hand. Now is the time. I know we have all tried to do this in the past, but the Spirit is calling for single-focused laborers. Do you really believe these are the last days before the Messiah will come again? Do you really believe in the depth of your heart it is soon? This is a test of faith to see if we will obey and seek the strength from Him to accomplish the task. He must receive all the glory, for only He is worthy.

We have gotten away from the basics and have allowed the distractions of this world to hinder us from pressing in deeper with our Lord. The Holy Spirit has revealed this question in my soul, "Are you hungering and thirsting for Me?" I said, "Yes, I think about You all day." The Holy Spirit then quickened in me that if I am hungry and thirsty, I would feast more. I would spend time in prayer in the morning and evening. He showed me that I eat at least three times a day on most days. When possible I would like to take my time at meals, but I am often in a hurry because of the "eat and run" training in today's society. We as Christians have done the same with God. We think if we spend 10-15 minutes with Him in quality time He is happy with us. If you spent that amount of time with your spouse or children, would you have a strong relationship with them? You may think so, but I know if I spent more time with the ones I love, then I truly could have that deeper relationship with them. Nowhere in recorded history has it been written of a man on his deathbed, "Gee, I wish I would have worked more." No, most of the time it's, "I wish I would have spent more time with the family." As Christians, I do not want to say on my deathbed, "I wish I would have spent more time with the Lord."

We say, "We want more of God," but then we speak or view ungodly things which keep us from drawing closer to His presence. It is being hypocritical when we speak of wanting more of God and then proceed to bring things into our minds that drive His Holy Spirit further from us. It's called sin, not entertainment. "What? Know ye not that your body is the temple of the Holy Ghost which is in you, which ye have of God, and ye are not your own? For ye are bought with a price" (I Cor. 6:19,20a). "Know ye not that they which run in a race run all, but one receiveth the prize? So run, that ye may obtain (win)" (I Cor. 9:24). The apostle is telling us to run the race to win. TO WIN. We must work and use all our strength and being, in this Christian walk, <u>to win</u>. "He that overcometh, the same shall be clothed in white raiment; and I will not blot out his name out of the book of life, but I will confess his name before my Father, and before his angels" (Rev. 3:5).

We have to quit being defeated and recognize who our God is and the power He has given us. We can never lose unless we give up. Many have given up the <u>pursuit of more</u> of His presence and power and truth and faith and charity. There is no beginning or end to our God. We should never be satisfied with our last taste of His goodness. We should want

more and more and more. The fire should burn in us to desire
all of Him. We have become satisfied when we should be
craving more. I see that Daniel was consistent to pray three
times a day even though His enemies knew they could catch
him. How many of us would love to receive revelations like
Daniel did? By the way, he was very successful in his
governmental duties as well. His job was not a hindrance to
his prayer life. We all have access to the same God as Daniel.
In fact, we have greater access. The point is that we have to
go deeper. We have to eat and drink more of the Holy Spirit.
We must be truly born again and let His Spirit burn in our
souls. "The spirit of man is the candle of the LORD, search-
ing all the inward parts of the belly" (Prov. 20:27).

The new life we were given when we repented and
accepted Jesus Christ as Lord and Savior must be demonstrated in faith and power. We know that the only way to
increase our faith is to read the true Word of God. "So then
faith cometh by hearing, and hearing by the word of God"
(Rom. 10:17). We must meditate on it daily, so that it goes
from the head to the heart. Have you ever had a Holy
Scripture verse jump off the page at you? The verse has a
deeper revelation into your spirit. It becomes more alive.
Your heart starts beating fast because the truth is going
deeper in your heart. We need more of that in our lives. I
suggest a more challenging Bible such as the King James
with an original Strong's Concordance to look up original
meanings as the Holy Spirit leads. This will make you read
slower and go deeper and meditate longer in God's Word.
It's a lot of fun when the Holy Spirit brings the Holy
Scriptures alive in your heart. Try it—it is exciting. (I've
been doing it for years.)

Let's get to the real basics. Are you truly born again and
do you have faith in God? "Jesus answered and said unto
him, Verily, verily, I say unto thee, Except a man be born
again, he cannot see the kingdom of God" (John 3:3). The

day you accept the Lord Jesus Christ as your Lord and Savior, you receive a new heart that sees things differently. Your life should have changed dramatically. You see eternity and things in this world as temporary. Your desire in this world should fade and the things of the Lord should grow stronger. You should be a different person. Now, you may be holding on to some sin in your life, but it will eventually fall by the wayside if you keep pressing into the deeper things of God. Some people may get rid of their sin quickly, but the point is that you must come out of your sins through His power. We are called to be holy. (We will cover that in another chapter.) Jesus did forgive you of all your sins, but you cannot remain in your sins. Most of all, after being born again, you should be falling more deeply in love with our Lord Jesus Christ. The love you have should be growing daily and growing stronger. As this love grows, your faith in God should grow. "And Jesus answering saith unto them, 'Have faith in God'" (Mark 11:22).

We must have faith in who our God is. Do you believe that our God can do anything? Do you really believe in the depth of your heart that He can do anything? Do you believe that He is in complete control of the universe? Many of us believe that God can heal us, but do we believe we can lay hands on someone else and have God heal them? "For where two or three are gathered together in my name, there am I in the midst of them" (Matt. 18:20).

Do you really believe that the Almighty God is watching over you? He sees you at all times. There is nothing hidden from Him, even the thoughts in our hearts. "Thus saith the LORD; Thus have ye said, O house of Israel: for I know the things that come into your mind, every one of them" (Eze. 11:5).

Do you know or realize that our God is waiting on us to be the people He has called us to be? "Bring ye all the tithes into the storehouse, that there may be meat in mine house, and *prove me now* herewith, saith the LORD of hosts, if I will not open you the windows of heaven, and pour you out a blessing, that there shall not be room enough to receive it" (Mal. 3:10). Do you believe in the depths of your heart that this is true? If you test God, He will pour out blessings in your life. He will take a little while to see if you are faithful in the small things, but do you really believe He wants to do this for you? Do you know the other hundreds of promises of God that He has spoken to any that will seek and hear? "Behold, *I will do a new thing*; now it shall spring forth; shall ye not know it? I will even make a way in the wilderness, and rivers in the desert" (Isa. 43:19) Do you really believe His promises? Do you know there are 452 promises in the Bible? I am talking about believing in our God and standing on all His promises. Jesus could not do miracles when there was unbelief. We have to start believing in our heart of hearts that the Word of God is true for us. (**Heart Truth**) The devils believe and tremble. We must act on what we believe.

I know we all have a measure of faith, but the Holy Scriptures tell us how we can believe more: Read more of the Word of God. Try meditating on these Holy Scriptures:

John 14:12-15

12   Verily, verily, I say unto you, He that believeth on me, the works that I do shall he do also; and *greater works* than these shall he do; because I go unto my Father.

13   And *whatsoever ye shall ask in my name*, that will I do, that the Father may be glorified in the Son.

14   If ye shall ask any thing in my name, I will do it.

23

15   If ye love me, keep my command-
        ments.

These are the Holy Scriptures that the Most High wants us
to receive into the depths of our hearts so that His glory can
be seen more on the earth. I am not thinking about riches
here. I am thinking about spiritual things here, so that the
glory of God can be seen in all the earth. Do you believe
that you can walk on water? Do you believe you could run
along beside a chariot? How about being thrown into a
lions' den or fiery furnace and surviving? Can God multiply
your food or have you eat poisonous things and live? If you
answer no to any of these questions, you did not believe the
Holy Scriptures that are written above. He said **GREATER**.
That means we will run next to a speeding car and witness,
fly next to airplanes and share the Gospel, and walk through
nuclear bomb fallout and not be affected. If you have doubt
or unbelief, you won't see these things. Those who have
faith will see greater things.

In these last days, we must remove the human limita-
tions we have placed on God. (He is bigger than you think
He is.) I know there are some that are reading this and have
doubts or say that God does not work this way anymore, but
Jesus wondered if there would be faith when He returned. I
pray that you will meditate on the Holy Scriptures above
and let them get deep into your soul and spirit, because they
are life and truth. They are heart truths that we need deep in
our heart of hearts. Some might believe that this is fantasy
or like a Santa Claus list, but we must become more sensi-
tive to the gentle breeze, the still small voice, the soft tug on
our hearts from our Beloved. We must have faith in God, the
Creator of the universe, that He can do anything He wants.
Nothing can hinder Him. If we will humble ourselves and
spend time with our Heavenly Father through Jesus Christ,
His glory will be seen in us. He is alive and He is on the

throne. Let His glory be seen today as we worship and give thanks in all things. The joy of the Lord should shine forth in our lives because His Spirit is in all those who call Him Lord Jesus Christ. We need to go deeper in faith. **<u>Go.</u>**

CHAPTER 3

DIVINE INFLUENCE

The word "grace" is a word that is very special to Christians. We know the song, *Amazing Grace*, and the scripture that reads, "For by grace are ye saved through faith; and that not of yourselves: it is the gift of God" (Eph. 2:8). The word humbles those who get a glimpse of true grace.

Let me first define what grace is not. Many of today's Christians think grace is God's willingness to let us sin. God somehow winks at our rebellion and sin. God knows that we are human and allows us to remain in our sin because we are saved by grace. May God have mercy on our souls because we have been deceived by the enemy about true grace. This meaning of grace, so that sin may abound, is not found in the Holy Scriptures. We have been saved by the divine influence (grace) placed into our hearts.

The world says that man is just an animal walking upright. Some Christians say we are only human and cannot overcome sin in our lives. Is there a difference between those two statements? No, they are both lies. Those who obey the Lord Jesus Christ are called the children of God and have the power to overcome sin and walk righteously before our Lord through the blood of the Lamb. It's your choice: obey or sin.

The world says that we are sexual beings and can't control ourselves. Some Christians say that they are acting the way God created them and can't help it. Is there a difference between those two statements? No, they are both lies. God has given us the family structure as His design for procreation. He also gave us self-control through His Holy Spirit.

I could go on, but the point is that we can't claim grace and continue in deliberate and willful sin. Deliberate and willful sin is called rebellion and it must stop before He returns. Ask God to remove the desire and repent of keeping any sin in your heart. If you really look deep into your heart, the besetting sin with which you struggle is in there because you want it. I know it hurts to see that you are holding on to a particular sin, but once you realize it, you can repent and ask God to remove it. It is ugly when we see some of our selfishness, especially when we think we have given our all to Jesus Christ.

Thank God for His grace, His divine influence, placed into our hearts. It has shined the light on our sin so we can ask for forgiveness and be set free from sin. This is how grace works. We did nothing to deserve that divine influence (grace), yet God placed it in our hearts to see His power transform us and give us another mighty testimony for His glory.

The meaning of *grace* in the Old Testament is "favor" and comes from the root word which means "to bend or stoop in kindness to an inferior" (Strong's Concordance). Is that not a great picture of a loving God in action toward us? The Creator of the universe stooped down in His awesome power to help us. He came in the flesh for us to be with Him once again. In the New Testament the word is translated "graciousness, of manner or act (abstr. or conc.; lit., fig. or spiritual; espec. **the divine influence upon the heart, and its reflection in the life.**" Wow! This has more power than just unmerited favor as we are taught today. This definition enlightens our understanding to the Holy Scriptures which, in turn, always brings more power to our lives. Let us examine the definition more closely.

Let us look at the words "divine influence upon the heart." The Word says in Ezekiel, "And I will give them one heart, and I will put a new spirit within you; and I will take the stony heart out of their flesh, and will give them an heart of flesh" (Ezek. 11:19). This is the cry of all of us who have been touched by the Spirit of the Living God. We want more of God in our hearts. We want to be consumed by His Holy Spirit. "Create in me a clean heart, O God; and renew a right spirit within me" (Ps. 51:10). We want more grace, and that grace is the divine influence in our hearts, not God's willingness to cover our iniquities. That was done at the cross. That work is finished. He paid for all our sins. If you have sinned since coming to Jesus, repent and sin no more. (That's what he told the woman who was caught in adultery in John 8:11.)

At some point in time you will hate the separation that comes between God and yourself, and you will stop sinning. Ask for the desire to be taken from your heart and God will do it, because His divine influence (grace) will come into your life and set you free. You cannot continue with sin too long, because your heart will become hardened and you will not be able to receive the divine influence (grace). It's like the children of Israel hardening their hearts toward God in the wilderness. If you still have the desire to be set free from your besetting sin, then your heart has not become too hardened.

We talk about the cross so much we forget that He rose again and is living in the power of the resurrection. He overcame and gave us the power to overcome. For some reason, the only time the power of the resurrection is spoken of is once a year at Passover. We should be speaking about it at all times. He rose from the dead, being seen by hundreds, and He has given us power over the enemy so that we can walk as kings and priests. A king commands and his words are the authority of the land. The priest has access to the altar and brings the needs of the people when he goes to the altar. That's who we are in Jesus Christ. We have the authority to bind and loose. We have the access to intercede for the lost and every need of others.

Have you received His divine influence into your heart, or is your heart cluttered with the cares of this world? Do you feel the soft wind (the Holy Spirit) blowing on your heart when He is moving? Do you catch the still small voice when He is whispering to you? We want Him to move us into the big things, but we will not listen to the small callings. We say that we want more divine influence (grace) into our hearts, but are we listening to the gentle tugs?

The rest of the definition of grace intrigues me because it is the fruit of divine influence. It is "the reflection in the life." This is powerful to understand that as more grace (divine influence placed upon the heart) is given, the more we reflect the light of Jesus Christ in our lives. The more grace is received and understood in our lives, the more our lives will reflect the glory of the LORD for others to see. I am going to share some scriptures, and the power of grace will come alive in a way as you have never seen before.

Ephesians 2:7-8

7   That in the ages to come he might *shew the exceeding riches of his grace* [divine influence into our hearts and the reflection of the life] in his kindness toward us through Christ Jesus.

8   For by grace are ye saved through

faith; and that not of yourselves: it is
the gift of God:

We are in the last days before He comes, and He wants to
show the exceeding riches of His divine influence. It is a gift
of God. This truth should make you want to fall on your
knees, give Him a huge hug and worship His greatness and
mercy that He has had on your soul. Your eyes have been
open to everlasting life with Him. Truly His influence has
touched all who call Jesus Christ, "Lord."

Romans 5:1-2
1   Therefore being justified by faith, we
        have peace with God through our
        Lord Jesus Christ:
2   By whom also we have access by
        faith into this *grace wherein we
        stand, and rejoice in hope of the
        glory of God.*

"The grace wherein we stand" is not in permissible sin. It is
with His divine influence that He has touched us. The faith
that we have witnessed is true, because He has come into
our lives and has shown us His love. We did not cause the
divine influence to come, but we did respond and not harden
our hearts towards Him. How much more should we
worship a magnificent God?

2 Corinthians 9:8
8   And God is able to make *all grace*
        abound toward you; that ye, always
        having *all sufficiency* in *all things*,
        may abound to *every good work*:

God is working to have more influence in your life that you

will be sufficient in **all** things. That word *all* means all. All. Not sometimes or 90% of the time. All things. And to abound to every (all) good work. What power and security to know that as we let more of His influence into our lives, all our needs and all our work will abound and be sufficient. That's a promise you can rest on and claim every day. Wow!

2 Timothy 2:1-2

    1   Thou therefore, my son, be *strong in the grace* that is in Christ Jesus.

    2   And the things that thou hast heard of me among many witnesses, the same commit thou to faithful men, who shall be able to teach others also.

Be strong in the divine influence into your heart through Jesus Christ. It's not saying sin more so that His grace will cover you. He is saying to let more of the Holy Spirit come into your heart so that you will shine as Jesus Christ shined.

2 Peter 3:18

       But *grow in grace*, and in the knowledge of our Lord and Savior Jesus Christ. To him be glory both now and for ever. Amen.

Grow in more divine influence in your heart. Keep your heart away from sin so that it does not become hardened before His return. The more one continues to sin, the more he or she will make excuses for their behavior and soon will try to justify it. At that point the believer does not think change is possible. That is when Satan has trapped us and our hearts have become hardened because we have denied the power of God. We come to believe that God cannot overcome our sin, but that is a lie of the enemy. The enemy of our soul has spoken unbelief to our hearts whenever we say the words, "I can't." Those words should never come out of any Christian's mouth. What is in your heart will come out of your mouth, so fill your hearts with truth. The Holy Scriptures say, "...With men it is impossible, but not with God: for with God all things are possible" (Mark 10:27). Read the next Holy Scripture:

Psalm 84:11

> For the LORD God is a sun and shield: the LORD will give *grace and glory: no good thing will he withhold from them that walk uprightly.*

He will deliver you from your sin because He wants the best for you. You have to get the sin out of your heart by letting more divine influence (grace) into it. He will receive the glory when you ask Him to take it out of your heart. It becomes another great and mighty testimony for His glory.

Proverbs 4:7-9

> 7   Wisdom is the principal thing; there-fore get wisdom: and with all thy getting get understanding.
>
> 8   Exalt her, and she shall promote thee: she shall bring thee to honour, when thou dost embrace her.
>
> 9   She shall give to thine head an *orna-ment of grace: a crown of glory* shall she deliver to thee.

It is great to see that as we seek wisdom (the mind of Christ), we get the reflection (ornament) of a crown of glory. Those who know the end of the story know that we give Him back all the crowns that we are given, because He alone is worthy to receive them.

Acts 20:32

> 32   And now, brethren, I commend you to God, and to the word of his *grace, which is able to build you up,* and to give you an inheritance among all them which are sanctified.

That divine influence gives us strength to stand, and we desperately need that in these times. In fact, in Hebrews 4:16 it says, "Let us therefore come boldly unto the throne of grace, that we may obtain mercy, and *find grace to help in time of need.*" We need more of the perfect and precious divine influence in time of need. How can we have access to the most powerful place in the universe and yet we rarely go in? That is part of our problem. Many times we think we can do it on our own and the reality is, we need more of His divine influence to do everything. Jesus said He only did what His Father showed Him. How we need to follow that example. Let us find more grace (divine influence upon the heart and its reflection of the life) in our lives—a **heart truth** if we ever needed one. Grace be unto you, my brothers and sisters. That means something very special when you understand the true meaning of grace. Let grace abound and **GO.**

CHAPTER 4

THE TRUTH

The Truth. There is only one and it is absolute. God
wants us to "know that man doth not live by bread only,
but by every word that proceedeth out of the mouth of the
Lord doth man live" (Deut. 8:3). "Ye shall not add unto the
word which I command you, neither shall ye diminish ought
[take away] from it" (Deut. 4:2). "Only take heed to thyself,
and keep thy soul diligently, lest thou forget the things
which thine eyes have seen, and lest they depart from thy
heart all the days of thy life: but teach them to thy sons, and
thy sons' sons" (Deut. 4:9). I know the promise that we shall
know the truth, and the truth shall make us free (John 8:32)
is true and unchangeable. I know that this is not my value; it
is the truth. We need to fall in love with the truth. "Jesus
saith unto him, I am the way, the truth, and the life…" (John
14:6). There is only one truth. This is an absolute truth. Our
"God is a Spirit: and they that worship him must worship
him in spirit and in truth" (John 4:24). This is not an option.
This is a pattern of worship and a **Heart Truth**.

We must seek and obey the truth. "He that saith, *I know
him, and keepeth not his commandments, is a liar*, and the
truth is not in him" (1 John 2:4). There is a responsibility

when you have found the truth. "Now therefore fear the LORD, and serve him in sincerity and in truth" (Josh. 24:14). We are to "let not mercy and truth forsake thee: bind them about thy neck; write them upon the table of your heart: so shall you find favor and good understanding in the sight of God and man" (Prov. 3:3-4). His truth will "continually preserve me" (Ps. 40:11). He will "lead me in his truth, and teach me: for thou art the God of my salvation; on you do I wait all the day" (Ps. 25:5).

We must study and rejoice in the truth. We must "only fear the LORD, and serve him in truth with all your heart: for consider *how great things he has done for you*" (1 Sam. 12:24). We must "stand therefore, having your loins girt about with truth" (Eph. 6:14), "but speaking the truth in love, may grow up into him in all things" (Eph. 4:15). We must "study to show thyself approved unto God, a workman that needs not to be ashamed, rightly dividing the word of truth" (2 Tim. 2:15). The Lord would say, "I have no greater joy than to hear that my children walk in truth" (3 John 1:4).

As you can see from the many Holy Scriptures quoted above, the truth is to be sought and found and walked in. We must restore the truth in our own hearts and treat it as treasure, for it is. The world cannot see it and cannot understand it. Our eyes have been opened to it, yet we have mixed man's wisdom with it. This cannot be so. God's truth stands forever. There is nothing to compare with or measure to it. It is His and His alone.

The truth is His Word. The Holy Scriptures are preserved for us in the Holy Bible. It does not change with the times. It does not need to be translated into easier words. The Word of God is not confusing and hard to understand. The solution is that to understand it, you must have the Holy Spirit open your eyes. You must have a hunger and thirst for the truth. This only comes from grace (divine influence upon your heart). Ask the Lord to put more truth into your life. He will do it because He wants you to know more of Him.

There are many in America who claim to be Christians, yet they have not read the four Gospels. If you are going to follow Jesus Christ, you need to read what He said and taught. In fact, when I come across new Christians, I tell them to read the four Gospels three times each before going elsewhere in the Holy Bible. I tell them to read a King James version study Bible because God's Word is not a novel. A good study Bible will have margins that explain the 15th century meanings of the words.

The Word of God should be read slowly and meditated upon daily. It is your life source. You cannot survive without reading it daily. Many satisfy their flesh three times a day by eating. How much more should you feed your soul? We should be spending time with the Lord more than once a day. We can make excuses all day about our schedules, but the question remains, <u>What are your priorities</u>? We must fulfill our responsibilities in the natural, but there is a lot of time we could make for the Lord, if we really wanted to. Turn off the radio when you are in your car. Turn off the television or computer and spend time in the Word. There is a strong warning in the Word about being caught up with the cares of this life.

Luke 21:33-36

33   Heaven and earth shall pass away: but my words shall not pass away.

34   And take heed to yourselves, lest at any time your hearts be overcharged with surfeiting, and drunkenness, and *cares of this life*, and so that day come upon you unawares.

35   For as a *snare* shall it come on all them that dwell on the face of the

whole earth.

36   Watch ye therefore, and pray always,
that ye may be accounted worthy to
escape all these things that shall
come to pass, and to stand before the
Son of man.

As we see, only His Words are going on forever. We must
have them in our hearts. Verse 34 tells us three things that
are coming upon us if we are not aware of it. Hopefully,
most Christians are not doing the first two. The one to be
careful with in our Christian walk is the cares of this life. It
is natural and normal to take care of our family and to do
well on our jobs. The danger is when you have made these
such a priority that you do not have daily time for the Lord.
He is a jealous God who wants us to be with Him. He wants
us to have fellowship with Him and the saints that are in the
local body (church).

Verse 35 tells us that a trap (snare) has been sent to
make you miss the return of Jesus Christ. God wants you to
be functioning in the Body of Christ when He returns. We
are all important to the Body of Christ. The brothers and
sisters in Christ can teach us things and we can teach them
things. We need each other more than we realize or want to
admit. In verse 36 we are to <u>watch </u>that we don't get caught
in this trap, and we should give thanks that He has had
mercy and grace for us to see these traps that are set before
us. We must make time to mediate on the truth that has been
set before us.

Psalm 19:7-10

7   The law of the LORD is perfect,
converting the soul: the testimony of
the LORD is sure, making wise the
simple.

8   The statutes of the LORD are right, rejoicing the heart: the commandment of the LORD is pure, enlightening the eyes.

9   The fear of the LORD is clean, enduring for ever: the judgments of the LORD are true and righteous altogether.

10   More to be desired are they than gold, yea, than much fine gold: sweeter also than honey and the honeycomb.

The truth must be sought after with all your heart but must be spoken in due season by the Holy Spirit. The time to speak the truth is now.

The example I set forth in the first chapter is a truth for the start of your witnessing. Do not use the <u>words of truth</u> that trigger the lies of the enemy in the unsaved. Here are the alternative words to use as you begin to witness:

INSTEAD OF...	**SAY...**
Jesus	Immanuel
God	Creator
Sin	Disobedience
Love	Lovingkindness
Relationship	Covenant
Born Again	Restore/New life
Cross	Tree

<u>But once you have revealed </u>Jesus Christ to them, make sure to use the key Words of Truth from that moment on. We must use the Word of God in the power that it is. We must hold up the mirror of the law that they may see that their own righteousness is as filthy rags. All the sins I am

about to describe can all be forgiven if individuals repent and ask for forgiveness. Please understand that Jesus Christ died for all their sins, but they must ask for forgiveness and accept His covenant through Jesus Christ. The Word of God is truth, and sometimes the truth hurts. But in the long run, it is what is best for us. Here are some of the word games the enemy has substituted for God's Word.

God's Word	Enemy's Lie
Adultery	Affair
Fornication	Pre-martial Sex (living together)
Lust	Just Looking
Rebellion	Independence
Drunkard	Alcoholic
Enchantments	Harmless White Magic
Anger	Blowing off a little steam (rage)
Idleness of Time	Entertainment
Observe times	Astrology/Horoscopes
Hatred	Racism
Bear false witness	Little White Lie
Revelers	Partiers
Slander	Gossip
Selfishness	Got to be myself
Strife	Pride

I believe that you see my point in the fact that the enemy of our souls twists words, just like he did in the beginning. Nothing has changed. He is still trying to twist words.

Fortunately, the Holy Scriptures are clear that if you do not come to the full knowledge of the truth, you will perish.

1 Corinthians 6:9-11

9 Know ye not that the unrighteous

shall not inherit the kingdom of God? Be not deceived: neither fornicators, nor idolaters, nor adulterers, nor effeminate, nor abusers of themselves with mankind,

10   Nor thieves, nor covetous, nor drunkards, nor revilers, nor extortioners, shall inherit the kingdom of God.

11   And such were some of you: but ye are washed, but ye are sanctified, but ye are justified in the name of the Lord Jesus, and by the Spirit of our God.

You can be set free, but you must not stay in your sins. He has deceived a whole generation in this country. We now have open worship of Satan, because people think Satan is good. Satan is evil! He is the embodiment or definition of evil.

2 Corinthians 11:14

14   And no marvel; for Satan himself is transformed into an angel of light.

There is only light or darkness in the universe. I have never found a gray area in the Word of God. It is either "you shall" or "you shall not." There is not any darkness in the true Light. You cannot be a little drunk or commit a little adultery. You cannot serve Him just with part of your heart. Our God wants all or nothing. You cannot be a little dead. You are either dead or alive. I can go on, but you get the point. We need to get back to the truth. We are trying to use logic and studies and scientific proof to show that God's commandments are true and just. We need to tell them that they are His commandments they are breaking and if they continue to disobey, they will go to hell. Yes, we need to tell people that if they continue in their sin, they will go to hell. Jesus Christ spoke often about hell. Their blood will be upon your hands if you do not warn them. We must show the light and not mix any darkness with it. Too many see Satan as good. We have "good witches" who practice "white magic" for good. Satan has deceived many. We must measure everything by the truth, which is in the Holy Bible.

The words we are using in the first chapter of the book are all found in the Holy Bible. We are using words that the enemy has not used to deceive the lost. They are still the words of eternal life. The Word of God has not changed. It cannot change. It will not change. God's Word brings life to those who will put it in their heart and will keep it there. The Words of God are the most powerful and awesome sound in the universe. They cannot be hidden. They cannot be silent. They can break the hardest of hearts. They are the foundation upon which all of creation is built. They can bring life where death once was. They can remove mountains and shake the heavens. Our faith just needs to believe in the power of His Word. His Words are eternal and shall not pass away. The Word (Jesus Christ) was made flesh and He dwells in our hearts. Speak the Word of truth and **GO**.

CHAPTER 5

BEAUTY OF HOLINESS

"Who is like unto thee, O LORD, among the gods? who is like thee, *glorious in holiness*, fearful in praises, doing wonders?" (Exod. 15:11). Holiness is who our God is, and it is what our God requires of each of us. We cannot be holy without the Blood of the Lamb: "Having therefore, brethren, boldness to enter into the holiest by the blood of Jesus, by a new and living way, which he hath consecrated for us, through the vail, that is to say, his flesh, and having an high priest over the house of God: Let us draw near with a true heart in full assurance of faith, having our hearts sprinkled from an evil conscience, and our bodies washed with pure water" (Heb. 10:19-22). He is talking to us about this life, not the hereafter. Those who have entered His presence know that we serve a Holy God. Our God is the only God who is called Holy. (Israel sees God as holy, only they have not fully recognized the Messiah as already having come). If you have made covenant with the living God of the universe, you know He is holy.

There needs to be a restoration of true reverence in our hearts of who our God really is. The word written to describe my Bible is "Holy." It is called the Holy Bible because it is the sanctified, consecrated and the perfect Words of God. If you believe there are errors in the Holy Scriptures, then your walk will have errors in it. It is a small thing for Him to keep His Holy Word accurate throughout the ages. Does the sun rise every morning? Do the oceans run out of their boundaries? Do the seasons continue in their cycles? We need to trust that our God has preserved His Words to this day.

I know this to be true because God's Words have brought new life to me and millions of others. *Holiness* means "being set apart and dedicated." That is who our God is, and who we are to be. We need to stop apologizing for our walk in holiness. I know that some have turned this part of the Holy Scriptures into legalism, but Jesus did say unto us, "That except your righteousness shall exceed the righteousness of the scribes and Pharisees, ye shall in no case enter into the kingdom of heaven" (Matt. 5:20). (**Heart Truth**). We have a higher calling that we must walk. If you have not walked in God's truth and holiness, repent from the bottom of your heart and go and sin no more.

There is a deep reverence when you grasp just how holy our Heavenly Father is. So many people today have such a perverted view of the Most High God. It's amazing that He does not destroy us all for the blasphemy of His Most Holy Name. Now is the time when He will restore the glory and power of His Most Holy Name. It is time to reverence the Holy One of Israel. "God is greatly to be feared in the assembly of the saints, and to be had in reverence of all them that are about him" (Ps. 89:7). When Christ comes in His glory and power, "it is written, As I live, saith the Lord, every knee shall bow to me, and every tongue shall confess to God" (Rom. 14:11). "That at the name of Jesus every knee should bow, of things in heaven, and things in earth, and things under the earth" (Phil. 2:10); and "At that day shall a man look to his Maker, and his eyes shall have respect to the Holy One of Israel" (Isa. 17:7). This lack of reverence to the Creator must stop now. You must see the power of the Name. God will not be mocked; time is short. God's authority is being restored in the Body of Christ, and the world will know that His name is holy. "Thus will I magnify myself, and sanctify [honor] myself; and I will be known in the eyes of many nations, and they shall know that I am the LORD" (Eze. 38:23).

Psalm 104:1

> Bless the LORD, O my soul. O LORD my God, thou art very great; thou art clothed with honour and majesty.

There is a beauty of God's holiness that is being shown to those who are pressing in to see His glory. We are starting to understand honor, majesty, excellency, glorious, and beauty. We should have a fear and reverence for our Creator. He is the giver of all life and the creator of all life. He is the most awesome, powerful, righteous and holy One in the universe. He is the Almighty. He is the Most High God. There is none higher. He does as He pleases and there is none that can sway Him. He gave us breath and to those that know Him as Father, He gave us new life. Who can stand before Him? Who can give Him counsel? Yet, this Most Holy and glorious God is calling His covenant people to a new place. He is revealing a new place for us to see His holiness and to see His glory. Our faces will shine like Moses' face because we will talk face to face with Him. We are being drawn there by the Most High God and He wants "only thy holy things which thou hast, and thy vows, thou shalt take, and go unto the place which the LORD shall choose" (Deut. 12:26).

"Know ye not that ye are the temple of God, and that the Spirit of God dwelleth in you?" (1 Cor. 3:16). Many

Christians know of the Holy of Holies. It's the holy place where the Ark of the Covenant was placed. It was behind a large veil in the tabernacle in the wilderness. The Ark of the Covenant was first called the Ark of Testimony in Holy Scriptures until Numbers 10:33: "And they departed from the mount of the LORD three days' journey: and the ark of the covenant of the LORD went before them in the three days' journey, to search out a resting place for them." This is the same path Jesus Christ took. He testified until He died. Then He showed us the new covenant under the blood. He then showed us the place of rest. The word *ark* means "to gather" and the word *covenant* means "to select or choose." So, basically the Holy of Holies was to be a place to gather His elect. It is also interesting what Moses said when the ark was lifted up in Numbers 10:35: "And it came to pass, when the ark set forward, that Moses said, Rise up, LORD, and let thine enemies be scattered; and let them that hate thee flee before thee." Jesus, our covenant, said, "and I, if I be lifted up from the earth, will draw all men unto me" (John 12:32). Truly, as we lift up Jesus in our lives, His enemies will scatter and His people will draw close to Him.

There is a place in Him that the Holy Spirit wants us to worship. In four places the Holy Scriptures tell us to worship or praise the Most High in the beauty of holiness. The word *beauty* is only used in the Holy Scriptures with this meaning in these four places. It means "decoration, beauty and honor." It is from the root word meaning "magnificent, ornament or splendor, excellency, glorious, majesty, glory, and goodly honor." *Holiness* in these scriptures means "a sacred place or thing, sanctity, consecrated, dedicated, hallowed, holiness, holy, saint, or sanctuary." This is awesome. He is decorating the saints to bring His glory in our worship and praise unto Him. "But thou art holy, O thou that inhabitest the praises of Israel" (Ps. 22:3).

The Ark of the Covenant had three things that were

placed inside of it. The only way to get into the beauty of holiness is to have these three things inside us. The manna represents the bread of life (Jesus): "Jesus said unto them, I am the bread of life: he that cometh to me shall never hunger..." (John 6:35). You must participate in communion with Jesus.

The second item was Aaron's rod that budded. It represented the Holy Spirit. You must have the Holy Spirit inside of you with fruit and life coming out of you. "The fruit of the Spirit is love, joy, peace, longsuffering, gentleness, goodness, faith, meekness, temperance: against such there is no law" (Gal. 5:22-23).

Third are the tablets of the law that were given by the Father but are now written on our hearts. To obey is better than sacrifice. All of this is under the covering of the Blood of Jesus on the mercy seat on top of the ark. These three events (accepting Jesus Christ as Lord through communion, showing the fruit of the Spirit, and obeying His commandments) in your life will allow you to enter into the beauty of holiness. See how important it is to keep sin out of your life? "Behold, the fear of the Lord, that is wisdom; and to depart from evil is understanding" (Job 28:28). Sin hinders us from worshiping in the beauty of holiness. We were created to worship Him. The reason for our existence is to worship Him.

Have you ever met anyone that does not like music? True, it might be different music than what we like, but everyone loves music. God wants us to leave the music that pleases the flesh and just worship Him. He does not want the music that concentrates on self. He wants the "blessing and honor and power and glory forever" music. The music is all about Him. He has given us His all. How much more should we give Him our all?

Here are the four Scriptures that show us that special place He wants us to go.

1 Chronicles 16:29

> Give unto the LORD the glory due unto his name: bring an offering, and come before him: worship the LORD in the beauty of holiness.

2 Chronicles 20:21

> And when he had consulted with the people, he appointed singers unto the LORD, and that should praise the beauty of holiness, as they went out before the army, and to say, Praise the LORD; for his mercy endureth for ever.

Praise goes before the battle. The praise is the strength from the Lord in order for the saints to overcome. Our Lord has won the battle. It is the foregone conclusion. Praise is given in every situation. Praise and worship is the willingness of your soul to surrender and bow to who He is. To truly worship and praise is to acknowledge His greatness and holiness. We fulfill the reason for our existence when we love and adore Him in our soul and body, with all of our heart, and all of our soul, with all of our mind, and all of our strength. (When was the last time you yearned and hurt to express your love to the Creator of your life with ALL your STRENGTH?) He is worthy of all we have. He is the MOST HIGH GOD.

Psalm 29:2

> Give unto the LORD the glory due unto his name; worship the LORD in the beauty of holiness.

Psalm 96:1-9

> 1   O sing unto the LORD a new song:

sing unto the LORD, all the earth.
2   Sing unto the LORD, bless his name; shew forth his salvation from day to day.
3   Declare his glory among the heathen, his wonders among all people.
4   For the LORD is great, and greatly to be praised: he is to be feared above all gods.
5   For all the gods of the nations are idols: but the LORD made the heavens.
6   Honour and majesty are before him: strength and beauty are in his sanctuary.
7   Give unto the LORD, O ye kindreds of the people, give unto the LORD glory and strength.
8   Give unto the LORD the glory due unto his name: bring an offering, and come into his courts.
9   O worship the LORD in the beauty of holiness: fear before him, all the earth.

The beauty of this psalm should be meditated in your heart for days.

Verse 1 – A desire He wants from all His people. He wants a new song in our hearts that is from the depth of our hearts. He wants us all to share the melodies with Him that He has put in us to praise and worship Him. I am not saying that we are all called to be professional songwriters and singers. We are called to worship and praise Him every moment of every day.

Verse 2 – Give Him thanks every day for the great salvation He has given us.

Verse 3 – Witness to those around you and share your personal testimony of some of the great wonders He has done in your life.

Verse 4 – Tells of who He is. How great is He in your life? This tells you how much He should be praised by how much you think of Him—a little or a lot, great or greatly.
It should be GREATLY!

Verse 5 – He is the Creator.

Verse 6 – Tells us again who He is. Who is His sanctuary now? Strength and beauty are to be there.

Verse 7 – We must give our whole being unto Him.

Verse 8 – Honor and bless His Name and give yourself and all you are to Him as an offering. It's time to lay ourselves on the altar so He may consume us and use us.
Verse 9 – When we have done all of the above, we can enter into the beauty of holiness (the decorated sanctuary He has made).

Watch out, world, 'cause here we come! The earth shall fear Him because He has come into His temple that has been built. This has been, "built upon the foundation of the apostles and prophets, Jesus Christ himself being the chief corner stone; In whom all the building fitly framed together groweth unto an holy temple in the Lord: In whom ye also are builded together for an habitation of God through the Spirit" (Eph. 2:20-22). "Know ye not that ye are the temple of God, and that the Spirit of God dwelleth in you?" (1 Cor.

3:16). This is a **Heart Truth**. The building is being done now, and we must finish the construction of the temple of God that is inside of us. We do not need any more visitations. We need the habitation of His Spirit and then the glory of our Lord Jesus Christ will be seen throughout the land. Let His Spirit enter in. **Go.**

CHAPTER 6

RELATIONSHIP

Ohne of the most talked about words in our society today
is *relationship*. We are bombarded by print, radio, and
television about how we can find, keep, establish, and enjoy
our relationships. These kinds of relationships mainly
revolve around us and our feelings. Unfortunately, most
everyone has experienced one or more bad relationships. So
when we talk about a relationship with God, non-saved
people do not have a strong desire to enter into another one.
They cannot trust or understand the faithfulness of our God.
It's like comparing an earthly father to our Heavenly Father.
It's not a good or fair comparison. The word *relationship*
does not have a clear and defined meaning and purpose in
our society. In this chapter we will look at the word *relationship* through the Holy Scriptures and define what it is.

I have noticed that the word *relationship* is not found
anywhere in the Word of God. This is important to understand because there is not a strong definition to rely on in
the Holy Scriptures. It's a man-made word that means
different things to different people. *Relationship* is a lot like
the word *believe*. So many people say they believe in God,
but we know by their actions that they are not serving God.

John 3:16 says, "For God so loved the world, that he gave his only begotten Son, that whosoever believeth in him should not perish, but have everlasting life." In this verse, *believe* is defined in Strong's Concordance as "to have faith, commit (to trust), put in trust with." That takes on a whole new meaning when you put the true definition in that verse. Again, I am not trying to change the Holy Word of God, but because the word in our society has been so polluted, we must use the stronger definition to bring back the original meaning.

James 2:19 says, "Thou believest that there is one God; thou doest well: the devils also believe, and tremble." Here we know the devils are not "putting trust with" God, but they do know there is a God and they do have respect for Him. Read the Holy Scriptures where the demons cried out in recognition of who Jesus Christ was (Mark 1:23, Luke 4:33, 8:29). They did not believe in Him, but they sure respected who He was. The word *believe* obviously has a different meaning in this context than in John 3:16. The point is that we must use words that are clear and precise. Hebrews 4:12 reads, "For the word of God is quick, and powerful, and sharper than any twoedged sword, piercing even to the dividing asunder of soul and spirit, and of the joints and marrow, and is a discerner of the thoughts and intents of the heart." The power of God's Word must not be taken lightly. "Ye shall not add unto the word which I command you, neither shall ye diminish ought from it, that ye may keep the commandments of the LORD your God which I command you" (Deut. 4:2).

I asked the Lord, "Since so many are familiar with the word *relationship*, what makes a true relationship work and grow together?" I thought it might be commitment, but that word is not in the Holy Scriptures either. The word *commit* is in the Word of God, but it is used mostly in context with sin and wickedness. So as I prayed, the Lord showed me the word *covenant*. Understanding covenant is the key to a deeper walk with the Most High God. This is something that God has established from the beginning and expects us to keep even unto today. Those who have accepted Jesus as Savior and King have entered into a covenant that should not be broken. We need to learn and meditate on the true meaning of covenant. It is an agreement entered into by two people. It's a solemn pledge of commitment. It is the promise of God to all who enter. Covenant means that the two parties stand together as one. Today's society would recognize it as an agreement that cannot be broken.

The first covenant that God made with man was with Noah in Genesis 6:18: "But with thee will I establish my *covenant*; and thou shall come into the *ark*, thou, and thy sons, and thy wife, and thy sons' wives with thee" (Ark of Covenant). After the flood, He made another covenant with the whole human race. "And God said, This is the token of the covenant which I make between me and you and every living creature that is with you, for perpetual generations: I do set my bow in the cloud, and it shall be for a token of a covenant between me and the earth" (Gen. 9:12-13). He put His bow from His throne room in the sky and only those who look up can see it.

The next covenant that our God made was with Abraham: "And it came to pass, that, when the sun went down, and it was dark, behold a smoking furnace, and a burning lamp that passed between those pieces. In the same day the LORD made a covenant with Abram..." (Gen. 15:17-18a). Strong's Concordance has a meaning of *covenant* as "the dividing of meat, or from the root word meaning to select." I know there are teachings that talk about blood covenant, but in our society we do not see or smell the slaughter of animals for an atonement of our sins. Jesus is the new covenant, and we are to partake of the new covenant at the communion table. "But now hath he obtained a more excellent ministry, by how much also he is the mediator of a better covenant, which was established upon better promises" (Heb. 8:6). We have better promises than the old covenant. That is when the Holy Spirit revealed to me that covenant is like an engagement. We have entered into an engagement with Jesus Christ or the biblical equivalent of being betrothed. We are not our own. We have been bought with a price. We have pledged a contract in truth for a future marriage. Are we not called the Bride of Christ? Isn't He returning to a Bride who is blameless and without spot or wrinkle? The reason it is an engagement is because we have received some of the promises of God and can act in the authority of His Name, but some of the promises are not fulfilled until He returns. Have any of us received our new bodies? No. Have we received the power to overcome sin in our lives? Yes.

In the true tradition of Hebrew marriages, the engagement is when the real celebration takes place. In the Holy Scriptures we see this in the betrothing of Rebekah in Genesis 24:53-54:

> And the servant brought forth jewels of silver, and jewels of gold, and raiment, and gave them to Rebekah: he gave also to her brother and to her mother precious things.
> And they did eat and drink, he and the men that were with him, and tarried all night; and they rose up in the morning, and he said, Send me away unto my master.

These guys had a feast that went the whole night. Basically, you were married when you said yes to the groom, even though it was not consummated yet. When was the greatest moment of your life? It should have been when you joined the family of God. You recognized your unworthiness and accepted the invitation from God to become part of the Bride of Christ. You took a vow and made covenant to live for Jesus Christ the rest of your days. This should have been when you were truly born again.

In biblical times, the groom in those days would then leave and go prepare a place for them. Sound familiar? Jesus said, "In my Father's house are many mansions: if it were not so, I would have told you. I go to prepare a place for you. And if I go and prepare a place for you, I will come again, and receive you unto myself; that where I am, there ye may be also" (John 14:2-3). The bride also did not know when the groom would return and take her away. Sound familiar? "Then shall the kingdom of heaven be likened unto ten virgins, which took their lamps, and went forth to meet the bridegroom" (Matt. 25:1). "But the wise took oil in their vessels with their lamps" (Matt. 25:4). "And at midnight there was a cry made, Behold, the bridegroom cometh; go you out to meet him" (Matt. 25:6). "And while they went to buy, the bridegroom came; and *they that were ready went in with him to the marriage: and the door was shut*. Afterward came also the other virgins, saying, Lord, Lord, open to us. But he answered and said, Verily I say unto you, I know you not. Watch therefore, for you know neither the day nor the hour wherein the Son of man cometh" (Matt. 25:10-13). Most of us have read and been taught this parable. I have concentrated on the wise virgins. (It does not take any effort to be foolish.) The wise will hear wisdom and keep themselves ready for that special day. They remain focused and have their first love in their hearts. The wise virgins understand the vows they have taken.

Vows were taken when you accepted this covenant. "When thou vowest a vow unto God, defer not to pay it; for he hath no pleasure in fools: pay that which thou hast vowed. Better is it that thou shouldest not vow, than that thou shouldest vow and not pay" (Eccl. 5:4-5). "So will I sing praise unto thy name for ever, that I may daily perform my vows" (Ps. 61:8). This reminds us that we must daily die to the flesh and serve the living God. If you have made vows that you have not performed, there is mercy and forgiveness at the altar. But go and perform what the Lord has put in your heart, "being confident of this very thing, that he which hath begun a good work in you will perform it until the day of Jesus Christ" (Phil. 1:6).

This explains a lot about why God hates idolatry. We are betrothed to Him, yet we are flirting with the world. I understand why it is one of the big ten. "Thou shalt have no other gods before me" (Exod. 20:3). Our God is a jealous God. He loves us so deeply that it displeases Him when we do not have all our heart devoted to Him. The Holy Bible is filled with scriptures in the Old and New Testament with God's hatred for idolatry. According to Strong's Concordance, an *idol* means "nothing." It can't be compared to such a Great and Mighty God as ours. The definition of *other gods* is "any person or thing made the chief object of one's love, interest, or aspiration." This could be your job, your hobbies, your sports interest, your television, your family. Take your pick; the list is endless. Anything that you put as number one in your life besides Jesus Christ is a false god.

When you're engaged, aren't your eyes only to one? Aren't your desires only to one? You only want to talk about one. Your every waking thought is only about one. Your heart is filled with only one. If you are not consumed with Jesus Christ in this manner, then return back to your first love. It is never too late.

I do not understand how the world has bachelor and bachelorette parties the week before they are married. Your heart should not have any desire for one more fling. It is confusion and brings doubt about one another's love before they consummate their marriage. The enemy wants to keep division in their hearts before they get started in their covenant with each other. When you are engaged, you cannot be unfaithful. You cannot commit a little fornication. It is sin. The children of Israel hardened their hearts during the engagement period in the wilderness and only two men were able to get to the Promised Land.

The covenant you made with the Most High God is a very serious agreement that you have vowed. It is never too late to repent and ask for forgiveness if you have broken your covenant. He is waiting on those who have strayed and wandered into the wrong field. He is calling. Do you hear His voice? Come into the fold because time is short and there are few laborers. Repent about what you have done and remember, "if any man be in Christ, he is a new creature: old things are passed away; behold, all things are become new" (2 Cor. 5:17). Satan wants you to remember your past, but God has forgotten it once you have repented. "But if we walk in the light, as he is in the light, we have fellowship one with another, and the blood of Jesus Christ his Son cleanseth us from all sin" (1 John 1:7). "Now the God of peace, that brought again from the dead our Lord Jesus, that great shepherd of the sheep, through the blood of the everlasting covenant, Make you perfect in every good work to do his will, working in you that which is well-pleasing in his sight, through Jesus Christ; to whom be glory for ever and ever. Amen" (Heb. 13:20-21).

When sharing about the Lord Jesus Christ with the unsaved, please share the significance of the covenant He has established with us. It was paid in full and with a great price. We have made covenant with the Creator of all. Let us walk accordingly. **Go.**

CHAPTER 7

LOVINGKINDNESS

Love. "For God is love" (I John 4:8b). That is who He is. The response from us is defined as, "This is love, that we walk after his commandments. This is the commandment, That, as ye have heard from the beginning, ye should walk in it" (2 John 6).

The word *love* has lost its real meaning in our society. People have such a warped view of the beautiful word that describes our God. It is one of His attributes of who He is. The world does not have the slightest clue of the purest form of love. The love from our God melts the hardest of hearts when planted by the Holy Spirit. It will change lives with only a drop inside the heart. The precious love of the Father towards His children is too great to describe in words, so our God demonstrated it. Those of us who are parents know the love we have for our children. How much greater is the love from our Heavenly Father who has birthed us?

I know this next statement has not been said much in the modern church, but you <u>can know</u> the love of God in your life. Let me repeat that, <u>you can know </u>the love of God in your life. How deep it is. How wide it is. How long it is. How far into the heavens it reaches. Now I know nothing can come between us and His love: "For I am persuaded, that neither death, nor life, nor angels, nor principalities, nor powers, nor things present, nor things to come, Nor height, nor depth, nor any other creature, shall be able to separate us from the love of God, which is in Christ Jesus our Lord" (Rom. 8:38-39). But many are confused in their believing. They do not believe that you can understand the love of God. The following Holy Scripture shows us we can.

Ephesians 3:16-20

16   That he would grant you, according to the riches of his glory, to be strengthened with might by his Spirit in the inner man;

17   That Christ may dwell in your hearts by faith; that ye, being rooted and grounded in love,

18   May be able to comprehend with all saints what is the breadth, and length, and depth, and height;

19   And to know the love of Christ, which passeth knowledge, that ye might be filled with all the fulness of God.

20   Now unto him that is able to do exceeding abundantly above all that we ask or think, according to the power that worketh in us.

Meditate on this Holy Scripture for a few days. Let this knowledge of His great love come into your inner heart. All the saints are to know this part of God.

The world believes that love is an emotional high and a physical touch. Love is so much more. Sometimes we base everything on an experience. We have to have the experience in order to believe. But experience produces feelings. All feelings are real, but they are not always good or right. I might feel like running into the person who pulled out suddenly in front of me, but that's not right. I might feel like going home in the middle of the day because I am having a bad day, but that's not right either. The point is, feelings come and go, but we must rely on the Word of God. We must do things that our feelings do not want us to do but that the Word of God says that we should do.

Many Christians are going by feelings and experiences and are not lining up with the Word of God. When you do not feel like doing what is right but you do it anyway, then you are living by faith. That is loving our Lord Jesus Christ by faith. The world needs to hear about the greatest demonstration of love ever seen. "Herein is love, not that we loved God, but that he loved us, and sent his Son to be the propitiation for our sins" (1 John 4:10). (Propitiation means atonement.) Such a beautiful word as love must be redefined in our witnessing.

I propose another word which God has preserved for us in these last days which will get the real message across to the unsaved in America. The word demonstrates the love of God and it is basically sharing Jesus Christ in power and glory. As you can tell by the title of this chapter, the word is "Lovingkindness." Jesus Christ is Lovingkindness. "But after that the kindness and love of God our Saviour toward man appeared" (Titus 3:4). Let me explain.

Lovingkindness is only found in the Old Testament. This is interesting because His lovingkindness was manifested in His only begotten Son, Christ Jesus. The definition of *lovingkindness* is "kindness, beauty, favor, merciful, mercy." The root word that it comes from means "to bow (the neck only) in courtesy to an equal." There is only one that the Holy Scriptures say that He is equal to because they are all one – Jesus Christ. Lovingkindness is used in the Word of

God 26 times. The number *26* means "the Gospel of Christ." It is exciting to see just how perfect the Word of God is. Instead of the word "love," which the world has confused the meaning of, we will use the word "lovingkindness" and restore the beauty and compassion of the greatest love of all time.

Read the following Holy Scriptures to see that Jesus Christ is God's lovingkindness.

Psalm 17:7

> Shew thy marvellous lovingkindness, O thou that savest by thy right hand them which put their trust in thee from those that rise up against them.

Who saves us and is sitting on the right hand of God? Our Lord Jesus Christ.

Psalm 36:10

> O continue thy lovingkindness unto them that know thee; and thy righteousness to the upright in heart.

How can we know God, only by our Lord Jesus Christ, who is our righteousness.

Psalm 40:10

> I have not hid thy righteousness within my heart; I have declared thy faithfulness and thy salvation: I have not concealed thy lovingkindness and thy truth from the great congregation.

We are to preach the Gospel to every creature. We cannot hide the light under a bushel.

Psalm 40:11
> Withhold not thou thy tender mercies from me, O LORD: let thy lovingkindness and thy truth continually preserve me.

He is the way, the truth and the life.

Psalm 42:8
> Yet the LORD will command his lovingkindness in the daytime, and in the night his song shall be with me, and my prayer unto the God of my life.

Who is the Morning Star? Our Lord Jesus Christ.

Psalm 48:9
> We have thought of thy lovingkindness, O God, in the midst of thy temple.

Who is in the middle of the temple? Our Lord Jesus Christ.

Psalm 51:1
> Have mercy upon me, O God, according to thy lovingkindness: according unto the multitude of thy tender mercies blot out my transgressions.

Who blots out our transgression in the new covenant? Our Lord Jesus Christ.

Psalm 63:3
> Because thy lovingkindness is better than life, my lips shall praise thee.

All I can say is, "How lovely our Lord Jesus Christ is!"

Psalm 69:16

> Hear me, O LORD; for thy lovingkindness is
> good: turn unto me according to the multi-
> tude of thy tender mercies.

There is only one who is good and He is full of mercy – our
Lord Jesus Christ.

Psalm 89:32-34

> Then will I visit their transgression with
> the rod, and their iniquity with stripes.
> Nevertheless my lovingkindness will I
> not utterly take from him, nor suffer my
> faithfulness to fail.
> My covenant will I not break, nor alter
> the thing that is gone out of my lips.

He is the new covenant and He bore our stripes, the Lord
Jesus Christ.

Psalm 92:2

> To shew forth thy lovingkindness in the
> morning, and thy faithfulness every night.

He is the Morning Star and He is called Faithful – our Lord
Jesus Christ.

Psalm 103:4

> Who redeemeth thy life from destruction;
> who crowneth thee with lovingkindness and
> tender mercies;

Who saved us from our sin and destruction and crowned us
with glory? Our Lord Jesus Christ.

Psalm 107:43
> Whoso is wise, and will observe these things,
> even they shall understand the lovingkind-
> ness of the LORD.

Have you got the revelation? Our Lord Jesus Christ.

Psalm 119:88
> Quicken me after thy lovingkindness; so
> shall I keep the testimony of thy mouth.

Keep His testimonies coming forth about our Lord Jesus Christ.

Psalm 119:149
> Hear my voice according unto thy
> lovingkindness: O LORD, quicken me
> according to thy judgment.

Who is coming back as judge? Who's voice do we hear? Our Lord Jesus Christ.

Psalm 119:159
> Consider how I love thy precepts: quicken
> me, O LORD, according to thy lovingkind-
> ness.

Who is the Word of God made manifest? Our Lord Jesus Christ.

Psalm 138:2
> I will worship toward thy holy temple, and
> praise thy name for thy lovingkindness and
> for thy truth: for thou hast magnified thy
> word above all thy name.

We are not talking about a coincidence here. This is all our Lord Jesus Christ.

Psalm 143:8
> Cause me to hear thy lovingkindness in the morning; for in thee do I trust: cause me to know the way wherein I should walk; for I lift up my soul unto thee.

We are to walk like whom? Our Lord Jesus Christ.

Jeremiah 9:24
> But let him that glorieth glory in this, that he understandeth and knoweth me, that I am the LORD which exercise lovingkindness, judgment, and righteousness, in the earth: for in these things I delight, saith the LORD.

This is all our Lord Jesus Christ. Who gets the glory? From whom are the love, righteousness and judgments coming? In whom did He delight?

Jeremiah 31:3
> The LORD hath appeared of old unto me, saying, Yea, I have loved thee with an everlasting love: therefore with lovingkindness have I drawn thee.

How are we drawn to God? By His love through our Lord Jesus Christ.

Jeremiah 32:18-19
> Thou shewest lovingkindness unto thousands, and recompensest the iniquity of the fathers into the bosom of their children after

them: the Great, the Mighty God, the LORD
of hosts, is his name,

Great in counsel, and mighty in work: for
thine eyes are open upon all the ways of the
sons of men: to give every one according to
his ways, and according to the fruit of his
doings:

It is all our Lord Jesus Christ.

So as we talk of God's lovingkindness to the unsaved,
we are talking about our Lord Jesus Christ. We need to talk
of His lovingkindness because the world needs to hear the
mighty compassion of our God. Judgment is coming to the
world very soon, and there is an urgency that we tell people
of the lovingkindness He has for all the world. He does not
take pleasure in the death of the wicked. Preach lovingkindness—the Gospel of Christ—and Go.

CHAPTER 8

CHANGING THE PAST

There seems to be a trend in movies and television shows where a person can go back in time and change the past so that the future is different. There seems to be an innate desire to change the past events so that our present situation is not so bad. We hate reaping what we have sown, but it seems unless direct intervention of our God comes, we do reap what we have sown. The lovingkindness of our God is great. He has provided a way for us to change our past. It is the same way He has changed us. He forgave us of all. Forgiveness is the greatest act of love that God has given us. It changed our being, our soul, our life, when God whispered in our hearts, "I forgive you. I forgive you of all your sins. You have acknowledged your sin, repented, and accepted My sacrifice of My only begotten Son. Your penalty has been paid and your sin forgiven." We cried because of the great love He has for us. His lovingkindness gave us a new beginning. It brought joy to a broken heart.

The power of forgiveness melts the most hardened heart. Forgiveness gives us the power to set people free, plus it releases us from any bitterness that may come in. We must remember that even on the cross, our Savior said, "Father, forgive them, they know not what they do" (Luke 23:34). Jesus also said, "And when ye stand praying, forgive, if ye have ought against any: that your Father also which is in heaven may forgive you your trespasses" (Mark 11:25).

Forgiveness must come from us readily and freely. We must forgive all who offend us. (**Heart Truth**). I am not talking about lip service. It must come from our hearts. Jesus told us the penalty when He said, "And his lord was wroth, and delivered him to the tormentors, till he should pay all that was due unto him. So likewise shall my heavenly Father do also unto you, if ye from your hearts forgive not every one his brother their trespasses" (Matt. 18:34-35). This may come as a shock to most, but the Holy Scriptures declare, "It is impossible but that offences will come: but woe unto him, through whom they come" (Luke 17:1). In Matthew 18:21-22, Peter questioned how long we were to put up with offenses from our brother sinning against us: "Then came Peter to him, and said, Lord, how oft shall my brother sin against me, and I forgive him? till seven times? Jesus saith unto him, I say not unto thee, Until seven times: but, Until seventy times seven." How beautiful is the answer from the living God? He forgives us every day of our lives.

Life is too short to walk around holding grudges. We must restore the love of the brethren back into the church. None of us chose to be born into our earthly family. We were given our parents and brothers and sisters by the Lord. We all learned to get along the best we could in our natural family. In God's family we do not just "get along." We must love one another. It's the second commandment of the two that Jesus Christ gave us. "A new commandment I give unto you, That ye love one another; as I have loved you, that ye also love one another. By this shall all men know that ye are my disciples, if ye have love one to another" (John 13:34-35). It is time to walk in the higher standard to which our God has called us. It is time to demonstrate the standard of the precious power of Jesus Christ that He g forgiveness. God is joining us back together as one family under God. "Greater love hath no man that this, that a man lay down his life for his friends" (John 15:13). We can never get to this kind of love without forgiveness in our hearts. (**Heart Truth**)

The power of forgiveness is not flowing among the brothers and sisters of Christ because of strife. Strife, which only comes by pride, truly grieves the heart of God. He sees His children not walking in unity with each other. Many have been offended by leadership, pastors, and others and have left churches with unforgiveness in their hearts. It has hindered their walk with God because of unforgiveness. The enemy used the offense to drive them from the church to which they were called. This is not good. The Body of Jesus Christ must remember the work that the Lord Jesus Christ has done on the cross for them. He forgave them of all. (**Heart Truth**) "Let the wicked forsake his way, and the unrighteous man his thoughts: and let him return unto the LORD, and he will have mercy upon him; and to our God, for he will abundantly pardon" (Isa. 55:7).

I know and understand that there are deep wounds and scars in our lives from some horrible offenses, but if we do not learn how to forgive from the heart, we cannot be free from the past. This is the gift that our Lord Jesus Christ has given us—to correct the past and give us freedom in the present. The power of forgiveness should be a demonstration of our God's love in this world. The world believes in revenge as the standard reflex to an offense. We should be ready to forgive as a reflex because of what our Lord has done for us. Did He heal the broken in heart and bind up their wounds? (Ps. 147:3). I know this is hard for many to do, but we must remember, "For if ye forgive men their trespasses, your heavenly Father will also forgive you: But if ye forgive not men their trespasses, neither will your Father forgive your trespasses" (Matt. 6:14-15). This is a truth that Jesus Christ taught. If you plan on never forgiving a certain person of an offense, you bind yourself and you become the one in bondage. Life is too short to harbor ill feelings because of people's offenses. I find many times the offense is only a misunderstanding. When the offense is revealed, we can see how the enemy was trying to sift us from having a close and deep covenant with that person. (When you have made covenant with God, you are in covenant with your brothers and sisters in the Lord.)

It is critical that you do not hinder your walk with our Lord Jesus Christ. I say this because if you are holding onto unforgiveness in your heart, it will keep you from a deeper walk with your Lord. "Therefore if thou bring thy gift to the altar, and there rememberest that thy brother hath ought against thee; Leave there thy gift before the altar, and go thy way; *first be reconciled to thy brother*, and then come and offer thy gift" (Matt. 5:23-24). Our Lord Jesus Christ wants all of our heart, and who is better to have our heart than He is? Trust Him. I know tears will flow, but the peace will come and His precious love will heal the wounds and restore the broken relationship into a new love and respect for that person. Trust Him and let forgiveness rule in your life. Remember, life is too short to let bitterness and anger stay around. When you forgive, you release that situation and offense into the Lord's right hand. He will be free to minister into the other person's life now because you've shown the power of His love by demonstration. From the heart you have been set free of the offense and joy will arise in your spirit.

We must recognize that unforgiveness is a tool the enemy tries to use all the time.

2 Corinthians 2:7-11
      7   So that contrariwise ye ought rather

to forgive him, and comfort him, lest perhaps such a one should be swallowed up with overmuch sorrow.

8   Wherefore I beseech ye that you would confirm your love toward him.

9   For to this end also did I write, that I might know the proof of you, whether ye be obedient in all things.

10   To whom ye forgive any thing, I forgive also: for if I forgave any thing, to whom I forgave it, for your sakes forgave I it in the person of Christ;

11   Lest Satan should get an advantage of us: for we are not ignorant of his devices.

We see that the Apostle Paul is teaching them to forgive so that the enemy does not get an advantage into the believer's heart. Unforgiveness causes division and once you start to see this pattern that Satan uses, you need to act in humbleness and forgive. Sometimes you may not even be at fault, but ask for forgiveness to reconcile and restore the unity of the brethren.

I want to make sure that everything is made clear on this subject of forgiveness. I am talking about forgiveness of trespasses and not about compromising biblical truths. Jesus forgave the woman caught in adultery, and it is one of the most touching and compassionate moments in the Holy Bible. Jesus Christ demonstrates the power of forgiveness in the act of mercy. Many people forget the last words he spoke to her: "Go and sin no more." He forgives, but our God does not compromise.

There are many stories in the Bible where forgiveness is given, but God never sanctions us to sin. Peter states,

"Seeing ye have purified your souls in obeying the truth through the Spirit unto unfeigned love of the brethren, see that ye love one another with a pure heart fervently" (1 Pet.1:22). The only way you can love fervently is if you do not have ought with your brothers or sisters. God does not want anything from you until you are walking in unity with each other. This is such an important principle that we restore back into the Body of Christ. Our hearts must become one. We must become one body and one church on the truths of the holy Word of God. (I am not talking about the unification of all religions that is happening under the banner of peace.) I am talking about all the churches that split because of offense or minor doctrinal issues. The ones I am talking about have the testimony of Jesus Christ and keep God's commandments. Those are the ones that must unite. These are the real saints that are preparing for His return. He is returning for one Bride, and we must unite and love one another. How else can we bring in the lost?

It is written, "By this shall all men know that ye are my disciples, if ye have love one to another" (John 13:35). The only way we can get to this point is by forgiving one another. It is a commandment, but it should be a reflex as we meditate more about the great forgiveness that was bestowed on us. It should be in our hearts and on our minds continually.

We have heard all the sermons on the armor of God in Ephesians. I find it interesting that the piece of armor that goes on our mind is the helmet of salvation. "And take the helmet of salvation, and the sword of the Spirit, which is the word of God" (Eph. 6:17). We are to remember the great salvation of our God. He delivered us from the pit of hell and forgave us of all. As you remember this great deliverance, notice what automatically happens. The individual wearing the helmet (covering the mind) will begin to use the sword (Word of God) and speak of the great and mighty things of the Lord. You will not be able to stop sharing about the great plan of salvation. The more you meditate on the glory of Jesus Christ as Savior of the world, the more you will speak of Him.

His forgiveness is for everyone, even your worst enemy. We must have a heart for the lost souls in our communities. He forgave us of all. We must forgive and renew our desire to share the grace and mercy He has put in our lives. We must demonstrate His lovingkindness by forgiving. Use this divine power of forgiveness and **Go.**

CHAPTER 9

FEAST OF CHARITY

Charity is a word that has not been as polluted in our society as much as others. It is a word that has a very deep and special meaning to those who have known the lovingkindness of the Most High God. Most of us would consider the meaning of this word as "giving freely without any strings attached." It truly blesses our hearts when we give freely. Even when unbelievers give, they have a good feeling inside. We are taught in this world that true love is a two-way street. That is the world's definition. However, we are not of this world. True charity (love) is a one-way street. Our God keeps giving and giving even when we do not deserve it. He gave His only begotten Son to die for us, so that we might have everlasting life with Him.

We have turned so much towards ourselves that we can't help others. That is not what true Christianity is. It's not about us; it's about the spiritual dead that are walking around us. We tell unbelievers to come to church as they are. We tell them not to worry about cleaning up their act and that God will do that for them. We just want them to come and humble themselves and repent. We say that God will do the rest. But then we tell God that we can't witness about

His Son until we study more or get all sin out of our lives—when we're perfect. God will cleanse your heart more as you do His work.

A powerful minister named Mark Shell (msministri@aol.com), who comes through our church each year, teaches a beautiful series about how you cannot use the anointing on yourself. If we take care of His work, He will take care of our needs. The anointing that God has given you is to be used for others, not yourself. We must get our eyes off of us and on the work and special calling He has put in each of our lives. Your divine place in life is exactly where He will use you to minister the Gospel. The most powerful people in God's Kingdom are His servants. "And he sat down, and called the twelve, and saith unto them, If any man desire to be first, the same shall be last of all, and servant of all" (Mark 9:35). "And whosoever of you will be the chiefest, shall be servant of all" (Mark 10:44). The definition in the Strong's Concordance of a servant is a "bond slave." You have made covenant with the Most High God, and you will do as He commands; otherwise, you are in rebellion.

Now I know the Holy Scriptures tell us we are called friends. "Henceforth I call you not servants; for the servant knoweth not what his lord doeth: but I have called you friends; for all things that I have heard of my Father I have made known unto you" (John 15:15). But the scripture right before it describes who friends are: "Ye are my friends, if ye do whatsoever I command you" (John 15:14). God is looking for faithful and charitable people to witness to this lost world—people who give of themselves without expectations in return. Will you be one? There is a call to charity so that His glory may come.

The most beautiful chapter about charity is in First Corinthians 13. Some of the newer Bibles have translated this as "love," but the true word to be used is "charity."

1   Though I speak with the tongues of men and of angels, and have not charity, I am become as sounding brass, or a tinkling cymbal.

2   And though I have the gift of prophecy, and understand all mysteries, and all knowledge; and though I have all faith, so that I could remove mountains, and have not charity, I am nothing.

3   And though I bestow all my goods to feed the poor, and though I give my body to be burned, and have not charity, it profiteth me nothing.

8   Charity never faileth: but whether there be prophecies, they shall fail; whether there be tongues, they shall cease; whether there be knowledge, it shall vanish away.

13   And now abideth faith, hope, charity, these three; but the greatest of these is charity.

It is obvious that the Holy Scriptures are talking about something deeper here than what we know as love. We cannot go through the motions of lip service when God is calling for our hearts to give everything. Just as our faith must grow, so must our charity. "We are bound to thank God always for you, brethren, as it is meet, because that your faith groweth exceedingly, and the charity of every one of you all toward each other aboundeth" (2 Thess. 1.3).

Charity is not just giving of money and time. It is the giving of our whole being and our hearts to one another. The word *charity* comes from the word *agapao*, which means "love, affection or benevolence. A love feast (feast of charity), dear love." What a definition. A feast of charity? That sounds like an abundant and overflowing of generosity and kindness. The overwhelming outpouring to charities after September 11th was tremendous. How much more should we do for the local body of churches? If the churches would unite under one another and pool their resources, we could meet the needs of millions and change the hearts of America. This is not just a far distant dream; this is a deep desire of our Lord Jesus Christ in these last days.

A feast of charity is what Peter was talking about in First Peter 4:8-9, "And above all things have fervent charity among yourselves: for charity shall cover the multitude of sins. Use hospitality one to another without grudging." There is a powerful word in this scripture that we need to grasp. Fervent. It is quite descriptive. It is a strong adjective with a distinct description of the kind of charity we need in our lives. Many people we see every day are perishing, and yet we do nothing. The abundance and overflowing words of life must come forth. The key is that we cannot achieve this by ourselves. We cannot do this in our own strength. We know faith grows by hearing the Word of God, but how does charity abound?

It can only come out of a pure heart. "Now the end of the commandment is charity out of a pure heart, and of a good conscience, and of faith unfeigned" (1 Tim.1:5). "Flee also youthful lusts: but follow righteousness, faith, charity, peace, with them that call on the Lord out of a pure heart" (2 Tim. 2:22). "Blessed are the pure in heart: for they shall see God" (Matt. 5:8). We must keep our hearts pure and undefiled before our God.

We cannot let anything ungodly into our hearts. We must only put His truth and righteousness in the holy temple of God. We must do as the following scriptures say in Colossians 3:12-14:

12   Put on therefore, as the elect of God,
      holy and beloved, bowels of mercies,
      kindness, humbleness of mind,
      meekness, longsuffering;
13   Forbearing one another, and forgiv-
      ing one another, if any man have a
      quarrel against any: even as Christ
      forgave you, so also do ye.
14   And above all these things put on
      charity, which is the bond of perfect-
      ness.

The pattern in the Holy Scriptures is written above. From Strong's Concordance, *bowels of mercy* means "pity or sympathy, inward affection plus tender mercy (from the spleen)." The spleen is regarded as the seat of various emotions and affects certain modifications in the blood. The sum of this is that the bowels of mercies starts on the inside of us with the washing of the Blood of Christ and His mercies. We must let the Holy Spirit create the strong urge from within to see people as God sees them. He sees the lost as sheep without a shepherd. He wants all people to come to the knowledge of Him. His lovingkindness keeps the humbleness of our minds because He has loved us first. Meekness is not weakness. It is inner strength on knowing who our God is and that nothing is impossible with our God. The next part of the Holy Scripture to put in our hearts is longsuffering. We know that those who wait on the Lord <u>shall</u> renew their strength. The key to this word is "long." We must wait. Then we must forgive as we learned in Chapter 8. When we have done this, we can put on charity, which is perfectness.

I know this word *perfection* makes many stumble in our society, but the glory of our God is shown in perfect love, which comes only out of a pure heart. I know the change in my heart came by the power of the Word of God when I first believed. I also needed to die daily to the flesh or I could not love my brother. "If a man say, I love God, and hateth his brother, he is a liar: for he that loveth not his brother whom he hath seen, how can he love God whom he hath not seen?" (1 John 4:20).

There is another place in the Holy Scriptures where the pattern for reaching true charity is given. This pattern is found in Second Peter 1:5-8:

5　　And beside this, giving all diligence, add to your faith virtue; and to virtue knowledge;

6　　And to knowledge temperance; and to temperance patience; and to patience godliness;

7　　And to godliness brotherly kindness; and to brotherly kindness charity.

8　　For if these things be in you, and abound, they make you that ye shall neither be barren nor unfruitful in the knowledge of our Lord Jesus Christ.

It begins with giving it all. All diligence must be accomplished in every area of our walk with God. The other steps, from faith to patience, all add to our character (having the mind of Christ). The next to last step is again the importance of brotherly kindness. Until we reach that, we can't go into the fullness of charity.

The word *charity* is used 27 times in the New Testament. (The same number of books (27) are found in the New Testament.) The number *27* means "Preaching the Gospel." How perfect is the Word of God. When we reach true charity in our walk, we are preaching the Gospel. We will demonstrate the power of the Gospel by living it. Our actions will speak even louder than our words. When you have reached this standard, then the fruit is produced. The word *knowledge* in verse 8 means "recognition, full discernment." The root word means "to know upon some mark, i.e. recognize; to become fully acquainted with, perceive."

John 17:3

> And this is life eternal, that they might know thee the only true God, and Jesus Christ, whom thou hast sent.

You will know God and become fruitful.

Col. 1:10

> That ye might walk worthy of the Lord unto all pleasing, being fruitful in every good work, and increasing in the knowledge of God;

I know people may not realize that, even though they have professed the Lord, our God wants more from us. He wants the fruit from His seed. "Verily, verily, I say unto you, Except a corn of wheat fall into the ground and die, it abideth alone: but if it die, it bringeth forth much fruit. He that loveth his life shall lose it; and he that hateth his life in this world shall keep it unto life eternal" (John 12:24-25). Our God is a fruit inspector. "Even so every good tree bringeth forth good fruit; but a corrupt tree bringeth forth evil fruit. A good tree cannot bring forth evil fruit, neither can a corrupt tree bring forth good fruit. Every tree that bringeth not forth good fruit is hewn down, and cast into the fire. Wherefore by their fruits ye shall know them" (Matt. 7:17-20). I do not want anyone to condemn themselves if at one time they bore fruit but are not producing now. The Holy Spirit says, "Every branch in me that beareth not fruit he taketh away: and every branch that beareth fruit, he purgeth it, that it may bring forth more fruit" (John 15:2). So let it be known: The purging is done and now is the time to bring forth the fruit. "Those that be planted in the house of the LORD shall flourish in the courts of our God. They shall still bring forth fruit in old age; they shall be fat and flourishing" (Ps. 92:13-14). So even if you are older and the joy of the Lord has waned, the season to produce is now. The harvest is great. The laborers are few. "Be patient therefore, brethren, unto the coming of the Lord. Behold, the husbandman waiteth for the precious fruit of the earth, and hath long patience for it, until he receive the early and latter rain" (James 5:7). We are the latter rain. This move of God is for everyone. I love the fact that He is calling us "precious." We have a special place in the Kingdom of God in that we get to be with our love, Jesus Christ, wherever He goes. We get to minister to the Lamb of God forever.

Those of us who love Him and have tasted of His goodness know what I am talking about. It is the greatest peace you will ever know. If you have not tasted, seek. "Ye have not chosen me, but I have chosen you, and ordained you, that ye should go and bring forth fruit, and that your fruit should remain: that whatsoever ye shall ask of the Father in my name, he may give it you" (John 15:16). He is calling.

Again we see a pattern in the written word:

John 15:4-8

4 Abide in me, and I in you. As the branch cannot bear fruit of itself, except it abide in the vine; no more can ye, except ye abide in me.

5 I am the vine, ye are the branches: He that abideth in me, and I in him, the same bringeth forth much fruit: for without me ye can do nothing.

6   If a man abide not in me, he is cast forth as a branch, and is withered; and men gather them, and cast them into the fire, and they are burned.

7   If ye abide in me, and my words abide in you, ye shall ask what ye will, and it shall be done unto you.

8   Herein is my Father glorified, that ye bear much fruit; so shall ye be my disciples.

The Word of God should be our daily bread. It should be like water to our flesh. Without the proper diet of the Holy Word of God, we cannot survive. Instead of the three hours of television or reading of novels or whatever consumes our time, the time for studying the Word of God is now. The only way to start producing fruit is to get His Words into us. It will bring much fruit to our Heavenly Father. The fruit is described in Galatians 5:22-23: "But the fruit of the Spirit is love, joy, peace, longsuffering, gentleness, goodness, faith, meekness, temperance: against such there is no law." We have the power to walk in perfect charity. He did not give us an unattainable goal. "But now being made free from sin, and become servants to God, ye have your *fruit unto holiness*, and the end everlasting life" (Rom. 6:22). We have holiness by the blood of the Lamb, and we have been set free from sin.

We have to walk in charity to produce the fruit our God desires from us. He wants all our heart, our soul, our being, our minds, our love and our strength. He wants all or nothing. The true charity He has shown us deserves all that we have. He deserves it all for His glory. We were created to worship, praise, serve and bring glory to the only One who is worthy of it. When we reach true charity in our hearts, we are the witnesses and the ambassadors we are called to be. Walk in charity and let His glory shine. Go.

CHAPTER 10

THE GROOM IS CALLING
✤

We have been chosen by the living God to be His Bride. What an honor and privilege to be chosen by the Creator of the universe. He wants all of us to participate, but some will not answer the call. It is a free choice. You can choose to say yes or no. The Holy Scriptures tell us of a great and awesome love the Almighty has for us. We can understand the love of Christ. We may not understand why He loves us, but He does.

It's kind of like my wife, Carol, whom I have been married to for 23 years, at the time of this writing. I know she loves me with a deep and unlimited love. I do not fully understand why she does, but I know she does. I have a deep and passionate love for her. I can't always put my love for her into words, but I try to show her every day, the best that I can. It's even better with Jesus Christ because His love is even greater than the earthly kind. My spirit has the peace and joy that can only come from being with Him. He is showing the Bride of Christ a deeper walk He desires with all of us. It is a deeper walk in true charity.

As we get closer and closer to the heart of God, we are being consumed with walking, talking and praising His Name. We can walk in the power of His Name. We have the authority to declare that," this is the confidence that we have in him, that, if we ask any thing according to his will, he heareth us" (1 John 5:14). But, "ye ask, and receive not, because ye ask amiss, that ye may consume it upon your lusts" (James 4:3). We must make sure our hearts ask only what the Father wants for us. Then, "whatsoever we ask, we receive of him, because we keep his commandments, and do those things that are pleasing in his sight" (1 John 3:22). "But let him ask in faith, nothing wavering. For he that wavereth is like a wave of the sea driven with the wind and tossed" (James 1:6). We must get rid of all unbelief so that we can see the great and mighty glory of the Lord work in the earth. When we take God out of the box that we have put Him in, we can believe. "Now unto him that is able to do exceeding abundantly above *all* that we ask or think, according to the power that works in us" (Eph. 3:20). The windows of heaven can now be opened into your life because your faith in God is unlimited.

Matthew 17:20-21

> For verily I say unto you, If ye have faith as a grain of mustard seed, ye shall say unto this mountain, Remove hence to yonder place; and it shall remove; and nothing shall be impossible unto you. Howbeit this kind goeth not out but by prayer and fasting.

He is referring to any stronghold or besetting sin in our lives. We can overcome it. "But without faith it is impossible to please him: for he that cometh to God must believe that he is, and that he is a rewarder of them that diligently seek him" (Heb. 11:6).

Does the Bride believe He is faithful? Of course she does. That is one of His attributes. He is faithful. "I will even betroth thee unto me in faithfulness: and thou shalt know the LORD" (Hosea 2:20). He is the most trustworthy God of all. His ear is listening. "Hear my prayer, O LORD, give ear to my supplications: in thy faithfulness answer me, and in thy righteousness" (Ps. 143:1). It should make your heart burst to "sing of the mercies of the LORD for ever: with my mouth will I make known thy faithfulness to all generations" (Ps. 89:1). His faithfulness is everlasting. "They are new every morning: great is thy faithfulness" (Lam. 3:23). Faithfulness in who He is brings great peace to our being. "And the heavens shall praise thy wonders, O LORD: thy faithfulness also in the congregation of the saints" (Ps. 89:5).

The Groom chose us. He put the divine influence into our hearts and let us see His beauty. He told us that He loves us with a deep and passionate love. His heart wants to be one with us. He forgives us of all our faults, and our love towards Him grows deeper and deeper. He has shown His lovingkindness and has demonstrated His undying love for us. He tells us how beautiful we are to Him, and again we do not understand why He chooses us, but we love Him more because of His choice. We were not deserving of such a great love, but He gave it to us anyway. He looks into our eyes and tells us of the plans to be with us forever. He has a special place where we can go to be intimate with the Mighty Holy Creator. He longs for us to prepare ourselves for His return. His every thought is on us. He is encouraging us all the time and compelling us to draw closer to His heart. He is very jealous towards us and only wants the best for us. He is telling us of writing His love in our hearts so that we will never have fear. His perfect love casts out all our fears. His hand will always be there to hold and guide us in all of our days. His love for us is hard to put into words. He would rather just show us His love by actions. We respond by singing Him a love song from our hearts. His touch can bring us to our knees. A small whisper of "I love you" brings tears to our eyes. His hand on our head makes us feel weak all over. His arms around us make us feel like we are one. We know His strength brings peace and security that all is well. The kiss on our neck brings chills to our soul. The Groom has us wrapped around His little finger, but He will not take advantage of our love. We do not have any desire to be anywhere else. Those who worship Him must do so in spirit and in truth.

Our spirit longs for the Groom's presence. Our anticipation for Him should consume us. The bride's passion is enhanced while she works and prepares for her Groom. Her every waking moment is on the Groom. Her soon-to-be husband is all she thinks about. Her husband is all she talks about. The Holy Bride of Christ should be utterly consumed with her coming Groom and that special day. Her heart yearns deeply for the lover of her soul. She is engaged and is soon to be married to the Holy Son of God. She should purify and cleanse herself for the coming day. She knows that "the Lord is not slack concerning his promise, as some men count slackness; but is longsuffering to us-ward, not willing that any should perish, but that all should come to repentance. But the day of the Lord will come as a thief in the night" (2 Pet. 3:9-10a). Her heart is filled with the joy of the Lord and nothing will hinder her on that day.

She is clothed in the righteousness of Christ and is without spot or wrinkle. The garment of praise has been put on and the veil has been torn away, and the new veil is Jesus Christ.

Hebrews 10:20-23

> By a new and living way, which he hath consecrated for us, through the vail, that is to

say, *his flesh*; And having an high priest over
the house of God; Let us *draw near* with a
true heart in full assurance of faith, having our
hearts sprinkled from an evil conscience, and
our bodies washed with pure water. Let us
hold fast the profession of our faith without
wavering; (for he is faithful that promised;)

God looks upon us through Jesus Christ and sees the
beauty of holiness because we are washed in His blood.
"...Though your sins be as scarlet, they shall be as white as
snow; though they be red like crimson, they shall be as
wool" (Isa. 1:18b). According to Revelation 1:14, "His head
and his hairs were white like wool, as white as snow; and
his eyes were as a flame of fire." This is a beautiful description that Jesus Christ has in His redemptive work. The very
hairs on His head are a reminder of the perfection of the
saints and the price that was paid for their salvation.

What a great and mighty God we serve. There is a voice
in the distance, "And I heard as it were the voice of a great
multitude, and as the voice of many waters, and as the voice
of mighty thunderings, saying, Alleluia: for the Lord God
omnipotent reigneth. Let us be glad and rejoice, and give
honour to him: for the marriage of the Lamb is come, and
his wife hath made herself ready" (Rev. 19:6-7). Are you
ready?

Being a Revelationer is a person who sees the people of
the world as lost and in darkness. We must look and see that
the harvest is ready and we are the laborers. The truths that
are written in this book are essential to your walk as a
Revelationer. These are all biblical truths for the Body of
Christ. They are not the only truths, but they will strengthen
our walk in our covenant with God. We must meditate on
these truths until they are in our hearts and spirits. We must
go deeper in faith as the time is getting shorter. We must

understand the divine influence in our hearts and the reflection of the life from it (grace). Seek the truth with an unquenchable thirst and hunger and never give up. We must worship the Lord in the beauty of holiness. His holiness is the sum of all His attributes. To see His holiness will make us stand in awe of who He is. We must be faithful in our covenant and meditate on His lovingkindness. Let forgiveness flow from our hearts and live in charity. You will be His Bride and will be ready for His return. To be a Revelationer is summed up in these words: Go and share the testimony of Jesus Christ and keep the commandments of God.

This is the time to have fun sharing God's plan of salvation in this country. This new and exciting way of sharing our testimony has been given to us by our Lord Jesus Christ. Rejoice and preach the Good News (the Gospel). The time is now to obey the first command that our Lord Jesus Christ gave in Matthew 28:19, **"Go..."**

TOOLS OF THE REVELATIONER

The following pages are some of the designs to be put on shirts, hats, ties, tote bags, and travelers mugs. You can see these designs in color at the following website: www.revelationer.com. Come visit the site. We will be adding new designs and slogans every month. The proceeds from the sale of these items, including this book, go to:

Revelationer Ministries
PO. Box 1640
Woodbridge, VA 22195

This is a non-profit organization created to support other ministries and ministers.

The artist who drew the designs is Jonathan Allen. He is a good and upcoming Christian artist who can be reached through the above address. Danny Dutch and Samuel Reynolds created the website.

Look for other books in the future about the Revelationer on our website or at your local Christian bookstores. The titles are listed below:

Heart Truths of the Revelationer
The Testimonies of the Revelationer
More Ways of the Revelationer

I am available to minister and teach your congregation about these new witnessing techniques. You may write or e-mail me at the above addresses. I pray the anointing will continue to be upon all who read this book . Let the fire within you go and produce the fruit that our Heavenly Father desires. May His grace (Divine Influence) grow and be established in all that you do. Look upwards for your redemption is drawing near. Praise be to the Most High God.

By the Servant of the Most High God,
Reverend Fred Rundell

SEE MORE AT

WWW.REVELATIONER.COM

GET THE ARSENAL AT

WWW.REVELATIONER.COM

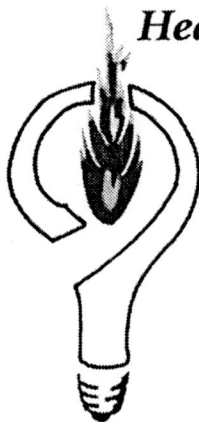

SEE MORE AT

WWW.REVELATIONER.COM

GET THE ARSENAL AT

WWW.REVELATIONER.COM

SEE MORE AT

WWW.REVELATIONER.COM

(Your Name)

GET THE ARSENAL AT

WWW.REVELATIONER.COM

ACKNOWLEDGEMENTS

The following people helped with the completion of this book:

My wife, Carol, and two sons, Bryan and Dan Rundell.

My Pastor, Dr. Tony Hall, and his wife, Brenda.

My good friends, Bob and Debbie Patten, Robert and Trudy Hrabak and their daughter, Veronica.

A special thanks to Diane Kuhns and her son, David Kuhns.

NOTES

The following three resources were used for definitions found in this book:

1. *Biblical Mathematics* by Ed. F. Vallowe Evangelistic Association, P.O. Box 826, Forest Park, Georgia 30051-0826.

2. *Funk & Wagnall's Dictionary.* Published in 1976.

3. *Strong's Exhaustive Concordance* by James Strong. Published by Crusade Bible Publishers, Inc., Box 90011, Nashville, Tennessee 37209.

Printed in the United States
908900004B

9 781591 605874